POLISHED

BY PRESSURE

Shining Through Upspoken Struggles

Dr. Nina R. Copeland

Visionary Author

Acknowledgements

To every soul who has ever dared to rise above what was spoken over them, this is for you.

Polished by Pressure is not just the work of one voice. It is a reflection of many hearts, shared stories, and hard-won victories. While I may have put these words on paper, the true spirit behind them belongs to all of us.

To my incredible coauthors: Latrese, Mark, Meg, and Lawrence, thank you. Your courage, your honesty, and your unwavering support helped shape this vision as it grew and gained its strength. In every moment of doubt, you reminded me that this message is bigger than us. Our stories, no matter how heavy or hidden, carry the power to set others free.

You are not just contributors. You are trailblazers, chain breakers, and light bearers. You chose not to simply survive, but to transform pain into purpose and pressure into power. You show us all that true leadership is born in those quiet, private battles and in the moments when we choose to keep going, even when no one is watching.

This book holds your strength. Every page carries the fire of your resilience, the beauty of your growth, and the clarity of your purpose. You prove that we are not defined by our past but lifted by everything we become along the way.

Together, we chose to speak what many still keep silent. We offered our wounds not as signs of weakness but as gifts of wisdom. We showed that the most powerful leaders are those who first learned to lead themselves through heartbreak, healing, and transformation.

Thank you for standing with me, for believing in this mission, and for reminding the world that *Polished by Pressure* is more than a title. It is living proof of what is possible.

My hope is that every person who reads these pages sees themselves in our stories and knows without a doubt that they too can rise! Stronger, bolder, and more radiant than they ever imagined.

Table of Contents

Introduction

There is a special kind of strength that reveals itself only under pressure.

Diamonds are formed deep within the Earth through intense heat and immense force. Pearls emerge when an oyster responds to an unexpected irritation. In much the same way, our most significant growth often happens when we are *pushed, tested,* and *stretched* beyond what we believe is possible.

But diamonds are not born polished or brilliant. Even after they form, they must be *cut, shaped,* and *refined*—sometimes even crushed, to reveal their true beauty and strength. Many of us have endured seasons that felt just like this: times so challenging that we questioned whether we'd make it through.

Yet, it is often those very moments that refine us. They strip away what no longer serves us and reveal the resilience and brilliance that were always within. These experiences don't break us; they transform us.

Polished by Pressure is more than a collection of stories. It is a testament to the courage, resilience, and transformation that live within each of us. These pages contain the real and raw experiences of men and women who have faced deep pain, shame, and disappointment, moments when giving up seemed easier than pressing on.

But these are not stories of defeat. They are stories of rising, of rebuilding from what once felt broken. They reveal the quiet strength behind each decision to keep moving forward, the silent battles that shape our character, and the tears that eventually become seeds of new life.

Through every chapter, we witness how we shed old versions of ourselves, only to emerge stronger and more authentic.

As a personal growth strategist and professional development expert, I know firsthand that true transformation does not happen in comfort zones. It unfolds in the uncomfortable, uncertain, and often painful spaces where we are forced to confront who we are and who we are becoming.

My work is rooted in helping people navigate these spaces with intention and courage. I understand the weight of silent struggles, the hidden fears behind confident smiles, and the difficulty of carrying heavy burdens while continuing to lead and show up for others.

When I developed the B.O.L.D. framework, it was not just a business or leadership tool. It became my lifeline, a way to reconnect with my true self beyond titles, achievements, and external expectations. I had to learn how to believe in myself unconditionally, make the most of what I had in each moment, release old limitations, and dare to step into new and unfamiliar territory. That same spirit of courage and renewal is at the core of every story in this book.

The individuals featured in *Polished by Pressure* have faced adversities that could have destroyed them. They've experienced embarrassment, shame, fear, and deep uncertainty. But instead of allowing those experiences to define them, they chose to rise and rebuild. Some created new visions, businesses, families, or identities. Others reclaimed their confidence, rediscovered their purpose, and renewed their faith in themselves. They turned setbacks into steppingstones, pain into power, and hardship into new possibilities.

This book invites you to look at your own life through a new lens. Reflect on the moments when life's pressures felt too heavy and consider that those very moments may have been shaping you into the person you were always meant to become. Honor every part of your story, even the ones you wish you could hide, because within them lies power and purpose.

Polished by Pressure is not a book to read once and set aside. It is an invitation to stand taller in your story and serves as a reminder that your value is not defined by what you have lost or the battles you have faced. It is defined by the way you continue to rise, rebuild, and lead with renewed strength and unwavering authenticity.

As you read these stories, I hope you feel seen, supported, and inspired. I hope you find the courage to keep moving forward, to trust your path, and to believe in the beauty of your journey. You are not alone in your struggles, and they do not define you. You are always *becoming* and through your growth, you inspire others to rise and build as well.

Let this book walk with you through your seasons of pressure. Let it remind you that these moments are not here to break you but to shape you into the leader and the person you are meant to become. You are not just surviving; you are *rising, building,* and *shining* in ways that will strengthen and uplift everyone around you.

Welcome to *Polished by Pressure*. May these stories give you strength, help you embrace your whole story, and aid you in moving forward with courage, grace, and an unshakable belief in your growth.

Dr. Nina R. Copeland, Visionary Author

International Speaker |Bestselling Author Retired Military Officer
Guiding leaders to embrace authenticity, break through limitations,
and lead with confidence and purpose

POLISHED BY PRESSURE

Relentless: Breaking Every Barrier

When I look back over my life, I see many versions of myself. Each version is shaped by experiences I never asked for but somehow needed. Every stage carries a piece of me forward, even before I understood what to lead truly meant.

People often believe that leadership begins when you earn a title, when someone finally calls you a "leader," or when the world chooses to recognize your strength. For me, leadership began much earlier and in much quieter places. It started in the hidden corners of my childhood, under the heavy weight of responsibilities that felt too big for a little girl to carry.

Leadership was never about a title for me. It showed up long before I wore a uniform, stood in front of a formation, or led a room full of people. It started with small, unseen sacrifices and unexpected responsibilities that shaped my spirit and molded my character.

As the oldest of five children, leadership was not something I chose, it was something that life handed me. No one called me a "leader," but I was already living it. I was labeled with words that left deep wounds. I was still a child, just trying to understand the world around me while toting burdens far too hefty for my small stature. The world does not give a child a guidebook on how to be the protector, the caretaker, and the strong one while still learning who she is.

Now, I understand those early experiences were not just childhood chores or burdens. They were the foundation of my leadership journey. They were the first ways I was polished by pressure, molded, refined, and strengthened to become the woman and leader I am today.

Those years taught me *resilience* in its rawest form. They taught me how to navigate chaos by being resilient, how to find light in the darkest places, and how to build strength from brokenness. Even in moments filled with silent tears and whispered prayers, there was a quiet determination within me. Something deep inside refused to believe that survival was the only story I was meant to live. I believed there had to be more, and I held on to that belief with everything I had.

Now, I know those versions of me were not separate chapters; instead, they were all connected, each preparing me for the next season. They taught me that leadership is not about standing at the front of a room but about standing firm in your truth when no one is watching. They showed me that true strength is built in silence, in sacrifice, and in the moments when it feels like no one sees or understands.

This is where I was refined by pressure, not in executives suites or on brightly lit stages, but in the quiet, hidden spaces where character is forged, resilience is born, and authentic leadership takes root. These unseen moments shaped me into the personal growth strategist and professional development expert I am today.

I learned early on that leadership is not just about guiding others. It starts with leading *yourself* through your darkest hours. It is about standing tall when everything inside you feels unsteady and is about showing up for others even while you are still healing.

The Power of Unseen Leadership

Growing up, my world was far from ordinary. When I look back now, I see a little girl lugging the weight of a fifteen-year-old at just nine. I had to grow up fast. My mind matured long before my age ever had a chance to catch up. I learned to watch closely, to read every room before I spoke, and to anticipate what others needed, even when they didn't say a word.

I experienced deep physical and emotional pain as a child. I saw things no child should ever have to see. The yelling, the tears, and the fear that made my heart race and shook my nervous system, those became a part of my everyday life. I still remember family members speaking negativity over my future, telling me I would end up just like my environment. They said, "I would get pregnant while young and would never become anything more than what they expected." As a child, all I could do was listen. Their words cut deep and stayed with me. It hurt so much to hear such defeat from the very people I loved and looked up to, the ones who should have protected and encouraged me.

Let me be clear: I was still a child, just trying to navigate a world that felt heavy and unpredictable. I was shaped by what was around me. I danced to music to drown out the noise in my mind. I argued when I felt misunderstood. I mirrored what I saw, because that was all I knew. But deep down, I was paying attention. I took mental notes even when no one realized I was watching.

Where I grew up, dreams were not expected to go far. They were small, simple, meant to help us survive, not thrive. The main goal was to get a job and just make it through.

While caring for my siblings, I learned to cook meals, dress them, and comfort them when they cried in the middle of the night. I still see us all circled in prayer every morning, hoping for a better day. I watched my friends play freely, laughing and living without a worry in the world, and I longed for that same freedom. But I learned early on that my journey was different. I had to be strong, even when I felt like falling apart. I had to show up fully, even when my own heart was breaking.

The ability to take command and hold things together began back then, long before the Army, long before any title. When my mom left the house, I stepped up. I gave the orders, kept things in line, guided my siblings, and call myself disciplined my siblings. Those early moments taught me how to make decisions under pressure, how to think fast, and how to keep everything from falling apart when the responsibilities became too overwhelming.

Because of what I saw around me; I did my best to shield my siblings from the storms we lived through. I chose to be their safe place, their protector, and the one who spoke life into them. Somewhere deep inside, I began hearing a small voice whispering that there was more to life than this. I decided to be an example for them. I knew I had to beat the odds, not just for myself, but for them, too. I wanted them to see that there was another way to live, that we did not have to keep repeating the same cycles we witnessed. I believed if they saw me rise above what was expected, they might believe they could, too. That belief became my fuel, my silent promise to them and to myself.

Through these small, quiet acts, I began learning what true leadership really looked like. True leadership is not about a label or talking in front of a crowd. It is about sacrifice, service, and showing up no matter what. Real leaders are not always in the spotlight. Many times, they are the ones serving in the background, holding families together, protecting hearts, and guiding others through storms no one else even sees.

Even as a little girl, I was already living out the foundation of leadership: service, sacrifice, and strength. I learned to stand up for the voiceless. I became the one who spoke when others were silent, the one who held space for those who felt unseen and unheard. I was the protector, the listener, and the one holding it all together, even when I felt like I was falling apart inside.

I carried burdens far too heavy for my small shoulders, and I carried them with a quiet strength I did not yet understand. Those moments of wiping tears, calming fears, and creating sparks of joy in the midst of chaos were shaping me from the inside out. I learned to lead with empathy, to stay steady in the middle of a crisis, and to find hope even when everything around me felt hopeless.

Those moments marked the beginning of my journey of being *polished by pressure*. What felt like unbearable weight was actually building my resilience, sharpening my emotional intelligence, and deepening my compassion. I did not realize then that every meal I cooked, every prayer I whispered, and every time I stood in the gap for my siblings, a leader was forming, who would one day stand strong in rooms I had not even imagined yet.

Those early pressures molded me. They prepared me. They taught me how to rise. They taught me how to see beyond what was in front of me, how to hold on to dreams nobody else could see, and how to keep believing in something greater.

This is what it truly means to be polished by pressure, not just surviving, but allowing the challenges to shape you, strengthen you, and prepare you to lead others with courage and grace. It was in those quiet, hidden moments that the real leader in me was born, the one who stands up for the voiceless and inspires others to do the same.

Rise Beyond the Environment

Deep down, I knew there had to be more to life than just making it through each day.

We didn't have conversations about owning businesses, investing, or seeing the world. No one encouraged me to think beyond my block, my circumstances, or what was directly in front of me.

This is called *cultural lag*—the gap between what is *truly* possible and what we have been *conditioned* to believe is possible. It keeps people playing small, blending in, and staying "safe," even if it means remaining stuck in the same cycles. I have watched so many people with incredible potential shrink under the weight of generational curses and unspoken expectations. These same patterns repeated again and again, keeping brilliant minds trapped in survival mode and self-doubt.

But church became my way out. It is the place where I caught glimpses of something greater and met people who believed I could do more. I remember one Sunday in Sunday School, we were asked to share what we wanted to be. I stood up and said that I wanted to become a police officer. After the service, a gentleman pulled me aside and told me, "You need to find a profession. A police officer doesn't require a degree."

At first, I laughed, thinking he was joking. But then, he looked me in my eyes and told me that it wasn't funny and that I was playing with my future.

That moment sparked something in me I didn't even know existed. For the first time ever, I realized I didn't have to just react to life, I could *design* it *on purpose.*

From that day on, I started planning. College became the first physical step in my new mindset and my safe haven. When I walked onto campus, I carried a sense of responsibility for my future. I was determined to complete college, so I did not play around in school.

I began dreaming bigger. I could become more than what I had seen growing up. I could build a life completely different from the one I was leaving behind. Therefore, I joined the Army to break free and began creating something for myself.

Joining the Army meant facing doubts and opposition from my family. But I kept going. I overcame the odds, commissioned as an officer, and tackled every challenge that military life threw at me. Leadership brought new pressures, but I met each one head-on until the day I retired.

Through every battle, internal and external, I kept rising. I learned that we are not defined by the environments we come from. We can rise above them, break the cycles, and build lives guided by purpose and courage.

That is what it means to be *Polished by Pressure*. Every limitation, every doubt, and every moment that tried to break me, refined me instead. Like a diamond formed under intense heat, I was strengthened and transformed.

I did not just survive. Instead, I became stronger, bolder, and more brilliant.

The Power of Reinvention

Choosing to join the Army was more than starting a new job, it was a declaration of a new identity. It was my way of rewriting the story I had been handed and proving to myself that I belonged in rooms and at tables I once thought were out of reach. The decision pushed me to meet new people, expanded my mindset, and stepped me into a level of discipline and growth that had shaped every part of who I was becoming.

The Army became the backdrop for some of my most significant transformations. It was where I developed into a strong, resilient woman; where I learned to lead and to serve; and where I became both a wife and a mother. The challenges of motherhood alone taught me patience, sacrifice, and how to nurture my family while staying true to my own goals and calling.

Military life was its own crucible. The physical training stretched my body beyond what I believed possible, but it was the mental and emotional challenges that truly reshaped me. The early mornings in the dark, the rhythm of boots hitting the pavement, and the discipline to keep moving even when every muscle burned forged a deeper strength within me. I learned to stand firm in uncertainty, to make split-second decisions that impacted lives, and to lead others through moments of fear and doubt.

As a African American female officer, I often found myself in spaces that were not built for me. Every day felt like a balancing act between showing up authentically and trying to navigate systems that were not designed with me in mind. I proved my worth repeatedly, while confronting deep-rooted stereotypes and unspoken biases. Some days, I felt invisible. Other days, hyper-visible, like every move I made was under a microscope.

Throughout my career, I stepped into leadership roles far beyond what I could have imagined as a young girl. I led teams ranging from 200 to over 5,000 people. I managed complex, multi-million-dollar contracts, oversaw critical budgets, and coordinated large-scale operations to keep entire aviation units mission-ready. There was no room for error. The stakes were high, and every decision I made rippled through countless lives.

I learned to cut through red tape, to advocate fiercely for my soldiers, and to trust my instincts, even when the path forward was not clear. These moments of leadership were often silent and unseen: spent late nights reviewing contracts line by line, early mornings walking the flight lines to check on my teams, and the small but powerful acts of care and support that rarely made it into reports or speeches.

These experiences solidified my belief that true leadership is not about public recognition or medals pinned to a uniform. It lives in the silent prayers whispered before tough meetings, in the quiet encouragement given to a soldier who feels alone, and in the unwavering presence you bring when everything around you feels unstable.

All of these moments, from early childhood lessons to the rigors of military service, are layers of pressure that did not break me. They refined me. They shaped me into the leader I am today: polished, resilient, and boldly standing in spaces I once only dreamed of.

A Call to Break Through

Because of my personal experiences, I know that many people, whether they realize it or not, are still trapped in childhood trauma. They may feel embarrassed or afraid to speak their truth, but they carry wounds they have never dared to say aloud. Many have learned to silence themselves, by choosing peace over honesty or seeking acceptance by putting everyone else first. They tote deep hurt that shapes how they show up in every space. Often, they hide behind roles and responsibilities, performing, striving, while silently battling the weight of their pain.

This is your invitation to break through. It is time to move beyond the walls you have built and step boldly into the life you are always meant to live.

My last major shedding of identity happened during my transition out of the military. It was abrupt, unexpected, and felt forced upon me before I was ready. That season revealed *the power of identity shifts* and made me want to become the person I needed when I was going through my own transition.

When I left the Army, I felt a deep stirring in my spirit to help others navigate their own turning points. I met so many women who looked unstoppable on the outside - executives, leaders, high achievers - yet beneath their polished exteriors, they felt empty and unseen. They were living lives defined by titles and roles, performing versions of success while slowly losing touch with their authentic selves.

I recognized that silent struggle because I had lived it, too. I knew what it felt like to be celebrated for achievements while weathering internal storms no one else could see. I knew what it meant to hold everything together for everyone else, while my own soul was crying out for rest, for healing, for a safe place to land. I understood the exhaustion of being the strong one, the dependable one, even when I felt anything but strong inside.

That is why I stepped into this next chapter. I want to guide women back to themselves, to help them remember the woman underneath all the titles and expectations. I want women to reconnect with the version of themselves that existed before the world told them who they should be.

I teach that real leadership is not confined to boardrooms or big decisions. It begins in still moments, when you choose to show up for yourself, when you decide to break the cycles that have kept you small, and when you finally say *yes* to your own healing and growth.

I have watched women come alive again. I have seen their eyes light up with new fire, heard their voices grow stronger, and watched their steps become more confident and grounded. I have witnessed them trade perfection for purpose, performance for presence, and fear for freedom.

Every time I see a woman break through, I am reminded why *my* journey matters. Every hardship, every victory, and every quiet moment of unseen leadership have prepared me to stand beside them and show them what is possible when you choose to live fully and boldly.

Now, I offer the same invitation to you.

It is time to reclaim your voice, step out of the shadows, and stop merely surviving. It is time to truly start living. It is time to lead yourself first, with honesty, with courage, and with unwavering belief in who you are becoming.

This is *your call* to break through.

Unseen leadership is the most powerful kind of leadership. It is forged in quiet moments, in the choices you make when no one is watching, and in the courage, you hold when there is no applause. It lives in the relentless spirit that rises again and again, no matter the setbacks or failures.

I did not arrive here by accident. I am the product of faith, grit, divine guidance, and an unshakable commitment to growth. I invite you to step into your power, to believe fiercely in your vision, and to break through every barrier that tries to hold you back.

Be relentless. Break every barrier. Embrace the strength of your unseen leadership.

And above all, **never stop becoming**.

Closing

My life is proof that you do not need permission to be powerful. You do not need a perfect past to lead. You do not need applause or validation to make a real impact. What you *do* need is the willingness to rise again and again, no matter what comes your way.

You are more than your résumé. You are more than your trauma. You are more than the roles you fill and the responsibilities you carry on your shoulders.

You are *a leader*, even if no one has ever spoken that word over you.

The power of unseen leadership is real. It is a kind of leadership that does not seek credit or recognition. It shows up through action, not titles. It is the kind that makes homes safer, workplaces stronger, and communities better.

I did not arrive here by chance. I am the product of pain, pressure, and promise. And if I can rise, you can, too.

This is your moment. Break free from the weight you have been carrying. Step out of the performance and let go of the need to prove yourself. Shatter every barrier that has tried to silence your brilliance.

Be relentless. Be bold. Lead without needing the spotlight and watch how your light transforms everything around you.

About the Visionary Author

A visionary leader, connector, and mentor, Nina is a retired military officer with over 21 years of distinguished service, dedicated to empowering individuals and organizations to shatter barriers and unlock their highest potential.

With a master's degree in Procurement and Acquisition Management and certifications from T.I.U.A. School of Business and the John C. Maxwell Team, Nina blends expertise in leadership, procurement, and personal development to deliver dynamic, results-driven coaching. Over her career, she has mentored, trained, and coached more than 10,000 Department of Defense personnel, cultivating resilient leaders capable of overcoming any obstacle.

Choosing to receive her undergraduate degree in social work, it is clear that a passion for helping others succeed has long been a focus for Dr. Copeland—something she has prioritized for many years. She also holds a master's degree in Procurement and Acquisition Management from Webster University, an honorary Doctor of Philosophy, and a Business & Entrepreneurship Coach Certificate from T.I.U.A. School of Business.

Dr. Copeland provides a relatable and accessible approach while still being thorough and well-planned. With over 21 years of hands-on experience working with individuals to reach their utmost potential, Dr. Copeland has the tools to guide others—because she has learned how to implement them for herself. Speaking of her own experiences, as a three-time best-selling author, an international speaker, and the founder of Copeland's Coaching and Consulting, Nina leads professionals and organizations through pivotal life transitions. Her innovative strategies drive personal growth, professional success, and lasting transformation. Rooted in the belief that success is a courageous journey, her work inspires bold action and resilience. Her latest book, *21 Day Transformational Journal: Unlock Your Boldness*, guides readers in self-discovery and unlocking new levels of achievement.

Outside of her professional work, Dr. Nina Copeland is a wife and a mother to three sons. Having raised a family and understanding what it means to advocate for the voiceless, she possesses a deeper awareness of supporting transformation in others. This is why she is so dedicated to her clients' success and outcomes—she cares about seeing people do well and inspiring them by leading by example.

How to Connect with Dr. Nina:
LinkedIn: Nina Copeland
Facebook: Dr. Nina Copeland
Instagram: @iamninacopeland
Website: https://iamninacopeland.com/

Meg Schmitz

Franchise Expert | Investor | Coach

Empowering women to embrace risks, seize opportunities, and thrive through entrepreneurship, resilience, and reinvention.

Polished by Pressure

This is the title of our anthology, and I wanted to give plenty of time to thoughtful reflection and introspection on what this means to me.

Polished.

I love polished silver, polished nails, and polished shoes—especially my high heels. I hate it when anything loses its shine, like my beautiful chandelier that looks like a scattering of fireflies. That shine isn't constant; it fades and fails to glisten as dirt, dust, and daily living take their toll. But hand me a rag and the right cleaning agent, and my silver, glass, and shoes are renewed. Mmm mmm... polished looks and feels so lovely.

Pressure.

Ugh, the word alone makes people shrink back and cringe. I used to hate pressure. It's usually self-created, but sometimes unforeseen demands are thrust upon my time and energy by outside forces. As an entrepreneur, I recognize that most of MY pressurized situations are self-inflicted. But learning how to work with time constraints and demands has helped me reframe pressure into something useful. Pressure makes things HAPPEN. Pressure makes things CHANGE. Pressure makes things BETTER.

Polished by pressure.

That's a whole 'nother thing. I'm thinking about lava blowing through a volcano, about volcanic ash and blazing heat, and the chemical reactions that turn ordinary earth and minerals into something extraordinary—like a gemstone. Without that pressure, the chemistry that transforms something unkempt into something beautiful and amazing wouldn't exist.

Let's embrace this title and truly think about how to leverage what might feel like a negative—and turn it into a positive.

Limitless Growth

I was at a conference in the fall of 2024, speaking on Women in Business and Empowerment. After wrapping up the fireside chat with my inspiring and amazing host, a woman approached me and asked how a woman *my age* (born in 1963, so I am 62 this year) still has fire and passion to continue opening new businesses and investing in start-ups.

(I freely volunteer my age because I don't feel it. I don't believe age is a barrier to further achievement. I don't think about my age as an energy index. I still have gas in the tank. I just think about how I invest in each day to get the best outcomes so I can reach my goals. And honestly, they get bigger every year. What will happen in the next 20? That's exciting to dream about.)

This lovely young(er) entrepreneur admitted she was exhausted from putting out "fires" every day. Any more than two, and she said she was *toast*. That sounded like a rookie problem to me, but we didn't have time to unpack why she called them "fires" or why they drained her so deeply. I know every day isn't glamorous, but I wanted to ask—what exactly about her business challenges was dimming her light?

I wanted to run back on stage, grab the mic, and say: *People… LADIES… you cannot put limits like this on yourself!* You can't stop your day because you're racking up failures or counting the misses as day-crushing problems. YOU are the entrepreneur. The buck stops with you! Conversely, I *highly* recommend ending your day with a celebration when you do something so amazing that it even surprises *you*. Throw a party. Sometimes the day's not over yet—and obligations may still be calling—but you deserve to celebrate "in the moment." Do that. Congratulate yourself. Then get back in the trenches.

Don't downplay the successes, and don't overinflate the failures. Find balance so you can continue.

You are driven to create and achieve. By joining the fray of business ownership, you've already invited problems, conundrums, problem-solving, and out-of-the-box thinking. You chose to start your own business—and people are watching. You don't need to be perfect. You just need to keep going. If you need to count backward to move forward, try the Mel Robbins Method: **5, 4, 3, 2, 1—Go!**

Even if you're not an entrepreneur, you're likely reading this for a reason—to find common ground with others navigating bold paths forward. You're here to draw strength from those who've overcome challenges, built resilience, and discovered new levels of empowerment. Welcome to the club. This life will stretch you, shape you, and challenge you to find clarity, purpose, and confidence.

You are being **polished by pressure.** Lean in. Let it reveal the diamond inside you.

Attitude

Over my six decades of living, I've learned a lot about attitude—and how it guides behavior. A negative attitude (especially those thoughts that loop through your head at night) can govern the energy you attract. Bad things happen to good people. Sometimes through our own choices. Sometimes not. But how you manage those moments is everything.

In 2018, I made an investment decision that seemed so right on the surface—but was all wrong underneath. The premise of the business was solid, but the CEO was manipulating the books and playing financial games. One day, he walked away, vanished, leaving me with no legal recourse to retrieve a multi-million-dollar investment. Gone.

That kind of defeat breeds doubt. Self-doubt.

Why didn't I see the signs? Why didn't I notice others in the industry keeping their distance?

I was so focused on the dream that I clouded my judgment with an idealized vision. I ignored the truth.

Two million dollars is a lot of money, no matter who you are. Despite the shock—both personal and financial, I had to decide how to respond professionally. People were watching. Employees. Franchise owners. Clients.

We still had bills to pay, events to manage, and obligations to meet. Life and business were moving forward, whether I wanted them to or not.

I couldn't treat it as a fatal blow, even though it stung for months.

I had to manage my reaction. I had to choose how to show up for those who remained.

I didn't feel fully present, but I poured everything from my conscious, positive self into helping others let go and move forward.

My best efforts helped me respond to critics and angry bystanders with the truth:

His actions were his. Not mine.

Celebrate The Win

Triumphs and victories are always more fun, they naturally fuel confidence. If you're like me and don't keep a running tally of the good stuff, the rewards can sneak up and surprise you.

In 2024, I had a strange year in business. Wins came in waves: long droughts, then heavy rains. No rhythm. The summer and winter holidays threw off my momentum. Then, at an industry conference in January 2025, I found out I'd reached Master Closer and Top Producer status. Just like that, I was walking among my peers with a new sense of belonging, I was a top-tier performer.

That sense of pride arrived fast and faded just as quickly. Business ownership keeps your feet on the ground. There's no resting on laurels. The name badge with the extra ribbons now hangs by my desk, reminding me I'm someone with skill and talent. But the second quarter of 2025 brought more bumps. March was magic. Then? Crickets.

Working for yourself means every day is an experiment in generating results. Dry spells can be discouraging. For me, moving forward takes mental and emotional gymnastics. I've trained my mind to banish doubt and negativity, but it's still work. I redirect my energy toward what matters. I remind myself to ask the Universe to conspire with me, not against me.

Celebrate the big victories but cherish the tiny wins too. Those are what keep your heart full, and your sails lifted.

Goal Settings and Outcomes

Personal honesty is key to showing up as your best self. But let's be real: it's hard to be honest with ourselves. I'm currently coaching one of our most capable employees. She's brilliant at what she does, yet deeply self-deprecating. She struggles to accept praise or set measurable goals.

Too often, women downplay their abilities. We doubt. We sabotage. Imposter syndrome has become part of our everyday language. Meanwhile, our bosses want us to aim higher, do better, and hit bigger numbers. So how do we grow when we're already battling self-doubt?

Forecasting can feel abstract. Many just wing it. I remember being jealous of the sales guys in the 1980s. They landed the big accounts while I was stuck with small names. I acted confident, but in reality, I constantly over-forecasted just to keep up. That wasn't strategy, that was desperation.

What I needed were KPIs. I needed baby steps. I needed a real plan to win.

And I had done it before. In my previous job, I crushed it—earning President's Circle in my first year. Maybe I was too young then to doubt myself. Back then, I didn't hear competition, I heard encouragement. But in my next role, I lost that spark.

I wish I knew then what I know now.

The Power of a Great Mentor

Since 2008, I've been in a Mastermind group led by a no-nonsense coach named Chad. Every week, he reminds us to show up like professionals, set goals, and follow through.

In 2013, Chad looked around the table and said, "You people can't get out of your own f*ing way! You ask for BIG, and then you aren't prepared when it arrives!" He was right. We were living on hopium— "I hope I hit my numbers... I hope the client says yes... I hope I don't get fired."

Then he added, "Don't you dare ask the Universe for something big and then not answer the door when it knocks!"

I was hanging on every word.

At that moment, the only goal I hadn't achieved was a successful marriage. I had the income. I had balance. I was self-supporting. But I'd been divorced twice. Twice. And both times, I'd fallen for narcissists in shiny packaging.

So, I made a list. A real one. Wants and needs. I worked on myself. I got honest. And by February 2014, I met Pete. Every date got better. Every box got checked. Chainsaws and black-tie events. Prairie life and boardrooms. A partner, not a competitor. Someone who respects and matches my success.

Thank you, Chad.

Take the Leap

So, what's the secret to success as a powerful woman? There isn't just one. But here's what I know: **Take the leap.** Even if the timing isn't perfect. Especially when it's not.

At that same 2024 conference, I heard a men's panel on women's empowerment. Three truths stuck:

- A man will apply for a job he's 50% qualified for. A woman will wait until she's 100%.
- Men want recognition for both masculine and traditionally feminine work. Women do both but often expect no praise.
- Men with kids keep climbing. Women with kids slow down "for the family," even if they're the breadwinner.

We are the change. We can't wait for empowerment to come from others—it must come from within.

You're feeling the pressure. That's why you picked up this book.

Let the pressure polish you. Let the fire shape you. Let the diamond emerge.

You're not just surviving. You're becoming something spectacular.

And I, for one, cannot wait to see what you do next.

About the Author

With over three decades of experience, Meg Schmitz has established herself as a dynamic force in franchising, angel investing, and entrepreneurship. Launching her first business at just 28, Meg's journey is a powerful example of resilience, reinvention, and the art of seizing new opportunities mid-career.

As a respected coach, consultant, and speaker, Meg is passionate about helping women overcome obstacles and step boldly into their power. In her session, she will share invaluable insights on how to take strategic, informed risks and confidently "take the leap" into new ventures and stages of life.

How to Connect with Meg:

LinkedIn: Meg Schmitz
Facebook: @Meg Schmitz
Instagram: @Meg Schmitz

Lawrence Stokes

Navy Veteran | Counselor | Bestselling Author | Life Coach. Inspiring others worldwide through writing, mediation, and personal growth leadership

.

Crunch Time!

At some point, you may have heard the term *"CRUNCH TIME."* If you're a sports enthusiast, you've heard that term is used on countless occasions. Crunch time is associated with those moments during a game when time is running out, the game is on the line, and the one person you know to be "clutch" is the one with the ball in their hands when time is winding down. That's the person who is cool, poised, and unshakable at the biggest moments. This is CRUNCH TIME—when it matters most.

For many, those moments bring intense pressure. Some people freeze or lose their ability to perform when the stakes are highest. They might do well under normal circumstances, but when it's crunch time, when the pressure builds, they disappear. You can't count on them. In other words, they're not the person you'd want with the ball in their hands as the clock runs out.

But that's sports.

Let's shift the focus and talk about life. When pressure builds, when there's no Plan B and failure isn't an option, can you handle it? Have you ever faced a moment like that? No backup plan. No safety net. Just you and the need to deliver. Let's talk about that.

Speaking from experience, I've faced moments of real pressure. I can say with complete honesty that, in my life, there was never a Plan B, and failure was never an option. I had to perform. I had to pull off what felt like miracles, even when I wasn't sure how things would turn out.

Pressure: The Young Father

As a newlywed and young father at twenty-one, with both of my parents gone by the time I turned eighteen, I had no reference point, no one to guide me on how to be a husband or a father. Still, I knew I had to protect my family. I had just completed my fourth year in the Navy, gotten married, and six months later, our first child was born. I knew nothing, only moving on instinct. What I did know was how I wasn't going to live, and that I would never raise my family in the kind of environment I came from. But how was I going to make that happen?

I never considered calling my other siblings. They were busy raising their own families and didn't need the burden of my struggles. Most of them weren't happy that I got married so young, and they definitely weren't thrilled that I hadn't asked anyone's opinion before I did. After all, I am the baby of the family. But like I said, they had their hands full and weren't in a place to worry about me.

Failure wasn't an option. I had no Plan B. I had to perform at that moment. I had to ensure the safety and well-being of my family. This was my CRUNCH TIME. There were times in my life that I did things. Not because I wanted to, but because I had to.

Pressure: The Traumatic Event

At my third duty station, with our family now grown to include a second child and living in a new city even farther from home, I faced one of the most traumatic experiences of my life and I faced it alone. I had to protect my military career while ensuring the safety and well-being of my family. It was a double-edged sword. A decision had to be made, and I had to perform during what was arguably the biggest moment of my life.

The details of that trauma still haunt me, but what I remember most vividly is the aftermath, the way it shifted the atmosphere in our home. My children, just three and two years old, could sense something was wrong. They didn't understand the situation, but they felt the tension, the fear, the uncertainty. It hung in the air like a thick fog.

The choice I faced was to confront the situation with force or allow it to play out while maintaining a protective environment for my family. I chose the latter. I saw how the event was affecting my children, even at their young ages. I witnessed the toll it took on my wife. I had to be the strength this family leaned on. There was no Plan B. I had to be at the top of my game. I couldn't let my family see me break, even though, during that time, I came dangerously close. Some days, I even contemplated suicide.

Those were the darkest days of my life. Every morning, I put on what I called my "soldier face," a mask of strength and confidence, while inside, I was falling apart. Be strong.

When I got home from work, my kids would run to me. I'd play with them, letting them feel like life was normal, like nothing was wrong. But I could tell they were worried about their mother. They could sense something was off. I worked hard to keep their focus elsewhere. I never let them see me at my lowest. I had no one to talk to, and I carried the weight alone, but I kept a smile on my face and did everything I could to preserve their sense of peace.

The evenings were the hardest. After dinner, after baths, after bedtime stories, when the house finally fell quiet, the weight would crash down on me, trying to figure out how to keep my family safe and my career intact.

Pressure: Starting Over

After being discharged from the military with nothing, despite serving nearly twenty years, I found myself once again in a situation where everything was on the line. I had to make sure my family was safe. We had just moved from California to Texas and were temporarily living with a family friend. We were neighbors in California, and our kids grew up together, but I knew this arrangement couldn't last. Tensions were building between their two daughters and my two sons, and I had to get my family out before that tension between the children spilled over to the adults. I had to remind my boys that this wasn't our home.

The transition from military life to civilian life was jarring. For almost two decades, I had worn the uniform, followed orders, and lived by a clear chain of command. Suddenly, I was in a world that I was totally unfamiliar with. I attend job fairs and I would see the resumes of people that never served and I felt so out of place. I only had military experience. I was often told before I got out of the military that finding a job would be easy, well that was not true, and those that told me that were still serving, and had yet to get this "civilian experience."

I had to find us a home of our own. An apartment wasn't an option. My sons were now teenagers starting high school in a new city, trying to adjust to unfamiliar schools, new faces, and a father who was struggling to find his footing. The pressure was crushing, not just financially, but emotionally.

I was fortunate enough to land a really good job traveling the country as a network engineer making enough money that I was able to purchase a home that my family could call their own. I was still in the probationary period of my job when I purchased this home, I took a gamble because once again there was no plan b. Then I got laid off, just 18 months after buying our home. At the same time, I began fighting the military over the nature of my discharge. I was trying to save our house while battling the system I had served faithfully since I was seventeen. I started out by contacting a few Senators of Texas, but got no response. Then I contacted one Senator, and she responded, and put me in touch with the military board of records, and from there the communication started. With every denial letter I received, I had a rebuttal in the mail the same day before the post office closed. I was prepared for a long, lengthy battle. My oldest sister told me I should hire an attorney, but I told her I didn't need one because I knew in my heart that I could win this battle.

And then, as if things couldn't get tighter, it was time for back-to-school shopping. I'm still unemployed, fighting the military. During a family discussion about school clothes, my oldest son looked at me calmly and said, "I'm not worried, Dad. You always come through."

Pressure. Crunch time. Just like a crowd waiting for something spectacular in a game, my sons believed I would rise when it mattered. I had never let them down before, and I wasn't about to start.

The next few weeks were a blur, but I didn't let them down. I managed to get them what they needed for the school year—and I kept fighting for my retirement. That fight wasn't just for me. It was for my family. I knew they would need medical care, dental care, and long-term stability. I didn't know how long I'd be without a stable job, but I knew I had earned that retirement. After giving nearly two decades of my life, I was not taking no for an answer, and each no I received, I returned another letter arguing my case.

Two years later, I won. My discharge was overturned and changed to retirement. Though I remained unemployed for the next five years, the supplemental income kept a roof over our heads. It wasn't luxury, but it was stability. It was security.

Failure was never an option. There was no Plan B.

The Polishing Process

I wanted to share with you just a few examples of the things that took place in my life where I was faced with extreme pressure, and in my mind, failure was never an option, and there was no Plan B. To take it a step further, I have always maintained that "quit was never in my blood," so I couldn't quit even when I wanted to. It wasn't in me to do so.

Through it all, this is where the POLISHING begins. This is where you look back over all you've been through and begin to think about all you've overcome. You gain self-awareness and understand that what you've been through were not only obstacles to overcome but lessons to be learned, and those lessons are the polish that makes you shine.

The Glass Shine Analogy

Let me use this "GLASS SHINE" analogy. If you've served in the military, you may understand this analogy, but if not, I'll make it easy for you. When preparing for inspection, your uniform had to look its absolute best from top to bottom, down to your boots. That meant your uniform had to be pressed and creased, creases so sharp you could split a piece of paper with them. And if you really wanted to impress, your boots needed that glassy shine.

I'd take the black shoe polish, add a bit of water to the lid, wrap an old T-shirt around two fingers, dip it in the water, then into the polish, and begin working in small, methodical circles. It was a slow process, sometimes hours of patient, repetitive motion. The first few layers always looked dull, almost muddy. But gradually, with each application and careful buffing, the leather would begin to transform.

Near the end, I'd take a lighter and gently heat the polish. The flame would melt the layers together, fusing them into a surface so smooth and reflective that eventually, the tips of my boots looked like glass, shiny enough to see your own reflection. Do you get the analogy?

Life's Polishing Process

There are times in our lives when we're faced with obstacles that seem insurmountable. As those moments unfold, we can feel the pressure rise. If you're anything like me, you're expected to perform, because failure was never an option, and there was never a Plan B.

But that pressure forged my shine. As I got older and began to reflect on my life and all that I had overcome, I realized those obstacles, those traumatic events, had prepared me for the version of myself I am today. They were the lessons I needed to learn. I firmly believe that many of the challenges we face in our youth are only glimpses of what's to come later in life. And if we're wise, we won't forget the lesson, we'll grow from it.

Think of it this way: the lesson repeats until it's learned. Have you ever experienced a situation that seemed to keep showing up in different forms? That's life trying to teach you something. Until you get the message, the pattern continues.

This is the polishing. The shine comes when you've learned the lesson, when you've overcome the obstacle and can anticipate the outcome if you ever face it again. As we grow older and face new situations, we become less reactionary. We take time to view things in their full context before responding. We place more emphasis on understanding and less on worrying about the result, because this time, we already have a plan.

Becoming Clutch

You've become the person with the ball in your hands during crunch time. You're calm, poised, and unshakable when the game is on the line—the one other look to when the clock is ticking down. That doesn't mean you won't encounter new challenges, but you've been forged under pressure. Nothing can shake you now that you aren't equipped to handle.

This transformation didn't happen overnight. It's the result of every sleepless night spent worrying about your family's future. It's every time you made a single dollar stretch until payday. It's every conversation where you stood strong even when you felt like falling apart. It's every moment when quitting seemed easier, but you chose to keep fighting.

Now, when adversity comes, you don't panic, you assess. You don't scramble; you strategize. You don't fear, you lead with confidence born from experience. You've been here before. Maybe not in this exact situation, but you've felt this pressure and you've risen through it victorious.

As we say, when someone has the hot hand and time is running out as soon as the ball leaves their hand... MONEY! COUNT IT!

Crunch Time

The truth is, we all face crunch-time moments in our lives. The question isn't whether they'll come, they will. The real question is whether you'll be ready: whether you've done the work, learned the lessons, and allowed the pressure to shape you into someone capable of handling whatever life throws your way.

Your crunch time may look different from mine. It might be a health scare, a financial crisis, a relationship challenge, or a career setback. But the principles remain the same: when failure isn't an option and there's no Plan B, you dig deep, rise to the occasion, and find a way through.

Remember, champions aren't made during comfortable moments. They're forged in adversity, polished by pressure, and refined by the heat of life's most demanding circumstances.

So, when your crunch time comes and it will, remember that you already have what it takes to succeed. You've been preparing for this moment your entire life, even if you didn't realize it.

The ball is in your hands. Time is running out. What are you going to do?

CRUNCH TIME.

About the Author

Born and raised in Bridgeport, Connecticut, Lawrence Stokes is a proud graduate of Central High School and a retired U.S. Navy veteran. He holds a Master of Arts in Professional Development with a concentration in Counseling from Dallas Baptist University in Dallas, Texas. He also earned a Bachelor of Science in Applied Science from the University of North Texas and an Associate Degree in Paralegal Studies from El Centro College in Dallas, Texas.

Lawrence is certified in Adult Conflict and Family Mediation and is also a certified Life Coach through Dallas Baptist University.

A prolific writer, Lawrence is the author and co-author of seven #1 bestselling books, including *Grief Through His Eyes* (Volumes One and Two), *King Conversations*, *Unleashed*, *In His Presence*, *Faith, Hope, and Love*, and his powerful autobiography *Ordered Steps*. He is also a contributing writer for *Own It* Magazine, where he continues to inspire others through his words and wisdom.

How to Connect with Lawrence:
LinkedIn: Lawrence Stokes
Facebook: @Lawrence Stokes

Mark Wiggins

Entrepreneur | Speaker | Author | Podcast Host
Empowering leaders worldwide through training, storytelling, and
motivational insights that inspire peak performance.

Polished by Pressure: The Comeback Is in You

There's something about pressure that reveals who you really are. It doesn't ask questions. It doesn't wait for a convenient time. Pressure just shows up, uninvited and relentless.

For me, the pressure came when I lost it all. Business gone. Speaking gigs, vanished. Clients, silent.

It was as if someone pulled the plug, and I was left standing in the dark, desperately trying to find the light switch.

I remember sitting in the silence of my home office, staring at my laptop, watching unpaid invoices and missed opportunities pile up. The man who had once spoken to thousands about success, mindset, and the power of your voice… was quiet. Broken. Stuck.

I had built a reputation as a speaker, author, and coach. I had published books like Permission to Succeed, Success Doesn't Need a Co-Signer, and later

King Conversations. I had platforms. Credentials. A story. But none of that felt useful when the bills were due and the phone stopped ringing.

And yet, somewhere deep within that pressure, something began to shift. The breaking point or the turning point?

What people often miss about success stories is the in-between. That stretch between falling and rising. I was caught in that space. And at times, it felt like I would never get out.

But I had a decision to make: either I would remain in the ashes of what once was, or I would gather what remained and start again.

That's what pressure does, it forces a decision. Will you fold? Or will you fight?

I chose to fight. And that's when the comeback began.

Let me share exactly how I made it back, a process I now call 3.5 Steps to Reclaiming Yourself Under Pressure. These steps aren't theory; they were born in the trenches of my own experience. And if you're walking through the fire right now, I hope they light your way.

Step 1: Permission to Heal, Permission to Hope

Before I could rebuild, I had to heal. That healing began with a truth I had written years earlier in Permission to Succeed:

"The only person who needs to give you permission... is you."

At the time, I wrote that line for others. Now, it was for me. I had to forgive myself for what went wrong, the missed signs, the bad partnerships, the moments I ignored my intuition. All of it.

What we don't talk about enough is how failure bruises your identity. And unless you pause to process that pain, you'll carry it with you into your next season.

Healing was step one. And with healing came hope. Not blind optimism, but the kind of hope rooted in the belief that I still had something left in the tank.

I gave myself permission to believe again.

Step 2: Rebuild with What Remains

Once the healing began, I looked around at what I still had:

- My voice
- My story
- My books
- My relationships

That was my foundation.

I reactivated my speaking platform. I started reaching out—not to sell, but to serve. I leaned heavily on the principles I laid out in *Success Doesn't Need a Co-Signer.* That book was built on the idea that you don't need validation to pursue purpose. You don't need applause to take action.

So, I stopped waiting for "perfect" conditions. I took *Off the Bench Magazine* to the next level. I dusted off old contacts and offered new value. I created products and experiences that could generate revenue—and more importantly, impact.

Everything I needed to get back up was already in me. I just had to activate it.

Step 3: Speak It Forward

One of the greatest lessons pressures taught me is this: your pain is someone else's blueprint.

In *King Conversations*, a powerful anthology I helped create, we brought together the voices of men who had battled through life's hardest moments. I didn't just publish that project—I lived it. I realized that speaking about my scars wasn't weakness—it was leadership.

So, I made it my mission to speak it forward. I began mentoring younger speakers. I trained professionals through my C.O.R.E. Speaker Training Program. I used my story as a teaching tool.

I went from silent and stuck… to bold and booked.

That's what pressure can do—it gives you a platform if you're willing to stand on it.

Step 3.5: Stay in the Game

Now, here's the half-step—the secret sauce. I call it 3.5 because it isn't a checklist item. It's a mindset. A decision you must make every single day.

Stay. In. The. Game. Even when it's slow. Even when it's hard. Even when the audience is small. You keep showing up.

There were days when I didn't feel like recording podcasts, writing emails, or making another phone call. But I did it anyway—not because I felt strong, but because I believed there was something on the other side worth fighting for.

Staying in the game meant redefining success. It wasn't about claps or cash—it was about consistency and calling.

The Diamond Effect

Here's what I've come to know: pressure doesn't just expose you; it expands you.

When I lost the business, I thought it was the end. But in truth, I was being refined, made stronger, sharper, and more intentional.

I came back better. More focused. More impactful. The platforms I've built since then are rooted in truth, not hype. Built on real resilience. Real lessons.

So, to every man reading this who feels like life is pressing in, hear me: you're not being buried. You're being built. You're not finished. You're becoming.

I've stood on big stages. I've been inducted into my college's Hall of Honor. I've coached athletes, trained executives, mentored youth, and led organizations. But none of that compares to the pride I feel from standing back up after being knocked down.

Pressure tried to silence me. Instead, it gave me a louder, more purposeful voice.

I'm still here. Still swinging. Still shining.

I'm out.

About the author

Mark Wiggins is a dynamic entrepreneur, acclaimed corporate speaker, and the Editor-in-Chief of *Off the Bench Magazine*. As the creator of the C.O.R.E. Speaker Training Program and co-founder of the Journey to Success Program, Mark empowers leaders and teams to unlock their full potential through high-impact training and development.

His expertise has made him a sought-after voice for Fortune 500 companies and global organizations, including Booz Allen Hamilton, Nike, the Jr. NBA, and the International Museum Store Association.

A prolific author, Mark, has penned *Permission to Succeed*, *Success Doesn't Need a Co-Signer*, and most recently, the powerful anthology *King Conversations*. He also hosts the widely popular podcast *Off the Bench with Mark Wiggins*, where he delivers motivational insights designed to inspire and uplift audiences around the world.

How to Connect with Mark:
LinkedIn: Mark Wiggins
Facebook: @speakerman87
Instagram: @OTBMagazine

LaTrese Rivers

Self-Taught Chef | Founder of A Plate of Love Catering

Serving clients for nearly five years with culinary excellence for private events and corporate luncheons, inspired by family, creativity, and a passion for food that brings people together.

Faith That Stands: My Journey Through the Fire

There's something about faith that doesn't make sense—until it's the only thing you have left.

I used to think faith was just about going to church, praying over meals, and trusting that things would work out eventually. But that definition fell apart the moment life knocked the breath out of me. That's when I realized: faith isn't just what you believe. It's what holds you together when everything else falls apart.

I didn't grow up with a silver spoon in my mouth. I grew up with prayer on my lips and struggle in my home.

My grandmother was the first person to teach me about faith. She had this quiet strength, always humming gospel hymns while stirring pots of greens, always speaking blessings over us kids before we left for school. Her faith was unshakable. I didn't understand it then, but I carried the memory of her prayers with me like armor I didn't know I'd need.

The first real test of my faith came in my early twenties. I had dreams—big dreams. I saw myself doing great things, walking through doors God opened just for me. But life didn't match the vision. Every time I took a step forward, it felt like something pulled me two steps back. Rejection letters, unanswered job applications, and nights spent crying in silence became my reality.

I questioned everything.

God, are You even there? Do You hear me?

One night, after another round of bad news, I sat on the edge of my bed and sobbed. I was tired, emotionally, mentally, spiritually drained. I opened my Bible, not because I was feeling holy, but because I was desperate.

My eyes landed on 2 Corinthians 12:9: "My grace is sufficient for you, for my power is made perfect in weakness."

I must have read that verse ten times. Something about it struck a chord in me. God wasn't asking me to be strong. He was inviting me to lean into Him.

That night, something shifted. I didn't have answers, but I had a flicker of peace. And that flicker would grow into fire.

Faith is funny like that. It doesn't remove the storm, but it gives you the strength to stand in it.

And storms came, oh, did they come.

There was a season in my life when I lost almost everything: a job I loved, a relationship I had invested in, financial stability, and worst of all, the version of myself I thought I had built.

I remember waking up one morning, staring at the ceiling, and thinking, This can't be my life.

I felt stripped bare, like God was allowing everything to fall away just to show me what couldn't be shaken. That's when I learned the difference between faith that speaks and faith that stands.

Faith that speaks says, "I believe." Faith that stands says, "I still believe—even now."

The hardest thing about that season wasn't the loss, it was the silence. When you're hurting, people will tell you to pray, to worship, to "keep the faith." But what happens when you do all that and still feel like heaven is quiet? That's when you find out whether your faith is built on convenience or conviction.

I wrestled with God. Not in a figurative way, I mean I literally argued with Him in the dark. "If You love me, why is this happening? Why does it feel like I'm being punished for doing everything right?" I felt like Job: stripped down, misunderstood, abandoned. But even in that mess of emotion, I kept coming back to Him. I didn't have perfect prayers, some nights, all I could whisper was, "Help me." And you know what? That was enough. Because faith isn't about having the right words; it's about having the right posture. It's about saying, "God, I don't understand, but I'm not letting go."

There's a kind of spiritual resilience that only comes from being broken and rebuilt. God didn't fix my situation overnight, He fixed me. Piece by piece, He began to restore what life had taken. He gave me strength even when I didn't ask for it. I started waking up with a little more hope each day. Not because my circumstances changed, but because I was changing. I was no longer depending on a perfect plan or timeline; I was depending on Him.

I began to see how the pain had purpose. How the closed doors were really divine protection. How the delays were building discipline. And most importantly, how the silence wasn't absence, it was sacred. God was doing His deepest work in me during the times I felt the most alone.

That truth became real during one pivotal night. I had been fasting and praying, not because I was trying to be super spiritual, but because I had nothing left to lean on. I remember crying out, "God, I'm tired of this wilderness. When will I see the promise?" And in the stillness of that moment, I heard, not audibly, but deep in my spirit, "When you realize I'm the promise."

That stopped me in my tracks.

I had spent so much time chasing purpose, people, and platforms that I missed the most important truth: God Himself is the prize. Everything else is extra. That realization unlocked a new level of peace in me. I wasn't waiting on a breakthrough to feel fulfilled. I wasn't measuring God's faithfulness by what I had. I was finally understanding that resilience isn't the absence of weakness, it's the audacity to trust God anyway.

After that, I started living differently. I moved with quiet confidence, not because life got easier, but because my roots went deeper. I learned to praise God even when the report was bad. I learned to encourage others while still bleeding myself. I learned how to carry both sorrow and joy in the same breath. That's faith that stands.

Let me tell you something that might free you: resilience doesn't always look like bold declarations and standing tall. Sometimes it looks like dragging yourself out of bed and whispering, "God, I trust You," through tears. Sometimes it's showing up to work when your heart is breaking. Sometimes it's staying in the room when walking away would feel easier. Sometimes it's just breathing—one inhale, one exhale—knowing He's still holding you together.

The journey of faith and resilience wasn't linear. I didn't "arrive." I still face moments that shake me. But I'm not who I used to be. The woman I am today has scars—but those scars are sacred. They tell the story of a God who never left. They testify of nights turned into mornings, of grief turned into glory, of ashes exchanged for beauty.

One of the greatest lessons I've learned is that faith doesn't eliminate struggle—it transcends it. It gives you the power to walk through the fire without being consumed. Just like the three Hebrew boys in the furnace, you learn that God doesn't always deliver you from the fire—sometimes, He meets you in it.

And if I'm being real, some of the most intimate moments I've had with God weren't in victory, but in surrender. It was in the brokenness that I found the blessing. It was in the waiting that I discovered my worth. And it was in the wilderness that I saw the wonder of His provision.

There came a moment in my journey where I had to decide: would I let my pain define me, or let God refine me?

For a long time, I walked around with invisible wounds. Smiling in public, bleeding in private. Saying "I'm blessed" while feeling broken. That's what many people don't talk about—the mask you wear when your world is unraveling, and you still have responsibilities, family, and people depending on you. But I reached a breaking point. And strangely, that was the beginning of my breakthrough.

One morning, I looked at myself in the mirror—not the makeup, not the hairstyle, not the curated version for the world, but me. The real me. And I whispered, "I don't recognize her." The truth is, I had spent years surviving. But survival mode had become my identity. I didn't know who I was outside of what I had endured.

But God did.

He began to show me the parts of myself I had buried beneath performance and pain, the parts that were creative, joyful, bold, and brave. He reminded me of promises I had forgotten, dreams I had buried, and gifts I had minimized. It felt like He was saying, "Daughter, you've always been more than what you've been through."

That's when the real healing began.

Faith became my foundation, not just during crises, but in my identity. I began to believe I was loved not because of what I did, but because of who I was. I stopped chasing validation and started walking in purpose. I stopped begging God for deliverance and began trusting Him for direction. I stopped asking, "Why me?" and started asking, "What now?"

The transition didn't happen overnight. Some days I still battled self-doubt. Some nights I still cried over what I had lost. But each time, God met me with grace. Each time, He whispered truth over the lies: You are chosen. You are called. You are seen. You are enough.

I began doing the work, emotionally, spiritually, and mentally. I went to therapy. I surrounded myself with truth-tellers, not just cheerleaders. I spent more time in God's Word than on social media. I created sacred spaces in my home where I could simply be, without pretense or pressure.

And slowly, I started to feel whole again.

I came to understand that resilience isn't about bouncing back, it's about rising transformed. I didn't want to return to who I was before the storm. I wanted to become the woman God was shaping in the midst of it. The woman who could speak life even while limping. The woman who could pray powerful prayers with a trembling voice. The woman who could help others climb out of the pit because she knew what it felt like to be in one.

That kind of strength doesn't come from self-help books or motivational quotes. It comes from being in the valley and realizing that the same God who walked with you on the mountain is there in the shadows too.

One scripture that became my anchor was Isaiah 43:2: "When you pass through the waters, I will be with you; and through the rivers, they shall not overwhelm you; when you walk through fire you shall not be burned, and the flame shall not consume you." That wasn't just poetic language, it was my life. I had passed through deep waters, and the fact that I was still standing was proof that God's Word does not fail.

And not only was I standing, I was standing stronger.

I found purpose in my pain.

Out of everything I went through, one of the most surprising gifts was how God turned my private battles into public ministry. People began coming to me for encouragement. They would say, "You just seem so grounded," not realizing that grounding came from first being uprooted. I began to realize that resilience isn't just for survival, it's for service.

Your scars become someone else's survival guide. Your testimony becomes someone else's lifeline. What tried to break you becomes the very thing that builds others.

So, I started speaking. I started writing. I began pouring into others what had once been poured into me. And each time I did, something in me healed a little more.

The thing about spiritual resilience is that once it's forged in the fire, you carry it with you. It becomes part of you—not as a defense mechanism, but as quiet strength. You don't flinch the same when the winds blow. You don't panic the same when doors close. Because you've been there. You've survived worse. And you've seen firsthand how God shows up, not only in the miraculous, but in the mundane.

One of the most beautiful lessons I've learned is that restoration doesn't always look the way we expect. For me, it didn't come with loud announcements or dramatic turnarounds. It came through steady grace. Through open doors I didn't have to force. Through connections I didn't chase. Through opportunities that fit like puzzle pieces I didn't know were missing. God began to unfold His plan, not all at once, but just enough to remind me that He hadn't forgotten.

And through it all, I started to walk differently, not arrogantly, but assured. I began to move with purpose, clarity, and peace. I didn't have to convince anyone of my worth. I didn't need applause to feel validated. I knew who I was and more importantly, whose I was. That kind of inner knowing is unshakable. It isn't built on titles, income, or followers. It's built on the unchanging character of God.

There's a peace that comes when you stop striving and start trusting.

I remember looking around one day at the life I had fought so hard to hold together and realizing that God had built something even better. Not just externally, but within me. I wasn't just healed, I was whole. I wasn't just standing, I was rooted. I wasn't just surviving, I was thriving.

I found joy again, not fleeting happiness, but joy that rises even on hard days. I learned how to celebrate the small wins, how to breathe in moments of calm without guilt, how to stop apologizing for my light.

That's what faith does. It frees you, not only from your past, but from the pressure to perform for your future.

I no longer fear failure the way I used to, not because I expect everything to go right, but because I trust that even when things go wrong, God can still use it. I've seen Him do it too many times to doubt Him now. Every delay, every detour, every heartbreak held a purpose. And every time I thought I had lost something for good, He either restored it or replaced it with something greater.

That's the faith I walk in now, not blind optimism, but anchored trust.

Here's what I know to be true: spiritual resilience isn't about never breaking. It's about rising after you do. It's about refusing to let the storm define your story. It's about standing firm when you have every reason to fold. It's about believing—when the evidence is nowhere in sight, that God is still good.

I've made peace with the fact that life will always bring challenges. I no longer pray for a life free from trials. I pray for the strength to endure them, the wisdom to learn from them, and the grace to grow through them. That's where the power is—not in avoidance, but in endurance.

Now, I live with intention. I pour into others the way I once needed someone to pour into me. I listen differently. I speak more slowly, love more deeply, and worship more freely. I don't just want to leave a legacy; I want to live it. I want my life to reflect God's faithfulness, not just in the mountaintop moments, but in the quiet ones, the broken ones, the ones no one sees.

To the woman who feels weary: I see you. I was you.

To the one holding it together for everyone else while quietly falling apart: God sees you. He is not absent. He is working, even now, in the silence, in the struggle. Don't give up.

Because one day, you'll look back, just like I did and realize that the season that almost broke you was actually building you. That the darkness was developing something sacred. That your tears were watering seeds of resilience.

And when that day comes, you'll know what I know now:

Your faith didn't fail. It stood. Even when you couldn't. Even when the answers didn't come. Even when the storm didn't stop. It stood.

And so did you.

About the Author

LaTrese Rivers is a self-taught chef and the proud founder of *A Plate of Love Catering*, a thriving private chef and catering company she has successfully operated for nearly five years. She runs the business alongside her supportive wife, LaShae Rivers, and dedicated business partners, Tenney and Tonyetta Sellers.

In addition to running her own company, LaTrese has worked as a chef in a variety of restaurants and has supported both restaurant owners and cafeteria managers in improving their operations. Her skill and professionalism have also earned her opportunities to cater large-scale corporate luncheons, showcasing her versatility and dedication to culinary excellence.

Inspired by her three brothers and six sisters, LaTrese credits her family as her greatest source of strength and motivation. Outside the kitchen, she enjoys singing and reading novels, always finding new ways to express her creativity and passion.

How to Connect with LaTrese:
TikToc: @A Plate of Love
Facebook: @A Plate of Love Catering & More
Instagram: @A Plate of Love Catering

www.ingramcontent.com/pod-product-compliance
Lightning Source LLC
Chambersburg PA
CBHW040838010826
48978CB00012BB/807